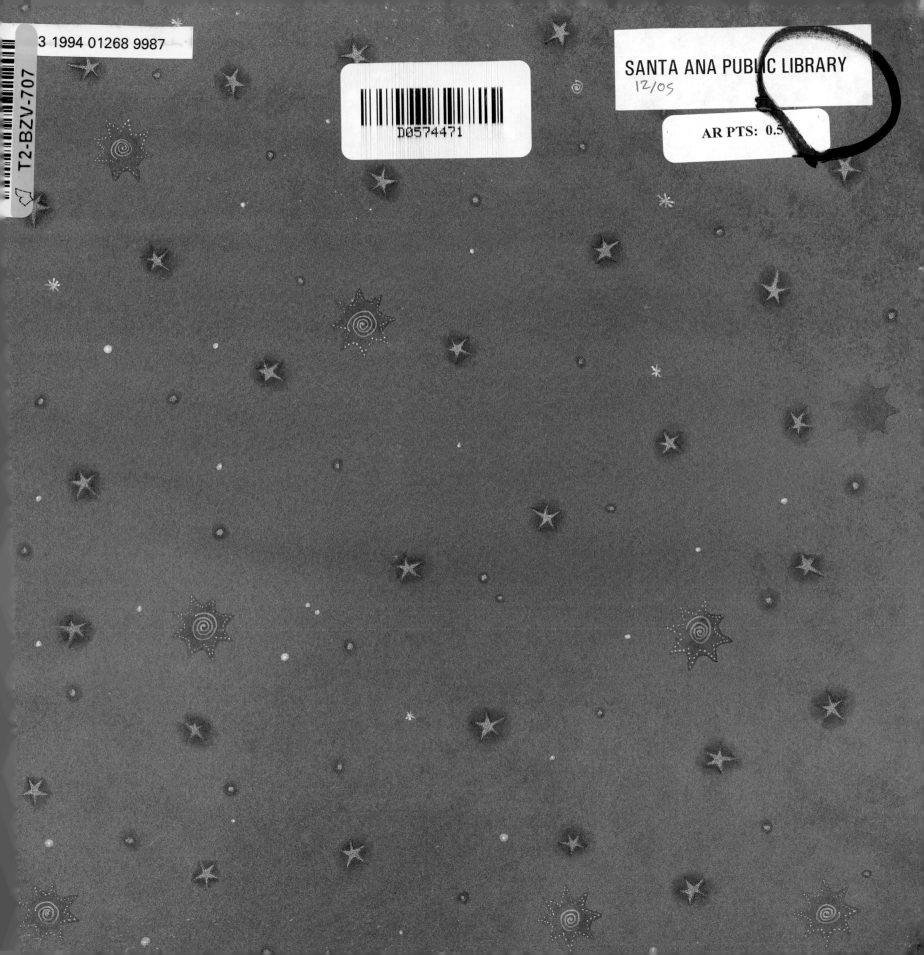

For John and Betty, their children,
grandchildren and great-grandchildren – B.D.

For John Minnion – J.R.

Jinnie Ghost

Berlie Doherty

Illustrated by Jane Ray

FRANCES LINCOLN CHILDREN'S BOOKS

Here comes Jinnie, the children call
but she doesn't turn her head, if she hears them at all.

Here comes Jinnie, as thin as the wind,
her hair as white as the feathers of owls.
Her eyes are like water,
her feet make no sound.
Here comes Jinnie, the dream-bringer.

Jinnie Ghost, Jinnie Ghost, where do you go?
the grown-ups ask, but the children know.

When the moon is round as apples,
that's when Jinnie comes.
The shadows are like velvet,
velvet houses, velvet horses,
that's when Jinnie comes.

She slides
through walls
She glides
up stairs
and into
the wildness
of dreams.

Charlotte sleeps
in a room full of toys.
"Dance!" whispers Jinnie,
and the creaking doors sing.
All the dolls come to life,
lion, teddy, clown,
they join hands and dance.

Charlotte creeps out of bed
in a princess's gown.

The curtain sways, and Jinnie has gone.
Jinnie Ghost, Jinnie Ghost, all the dolls call
but she doesn't turn her head, if she hears them at all.

Amy's carpet bubbles
with frogs and newts and toads.
Her sheets are spiders' webs
and her cat is black as night.

She steps out of bed
and rides a broomstick to Mars.
Her hair streams like comets' tails.

In a shower of falling stars
Jinnie shimmers by.

Jinnie Ghost, Jinnie Ghost, where do you go?

Tommy's room
is a whispering forest
and there in the moonlight
a unicorn stands.
Ride him! Jinnie laughs.

As Tommy gallops
to the end of the world
he sees a rush of leaves
where no wind has been
and Jinnie Ghost
has gone.

Jinnie Ghost! Jinnie Ghost! the unicorn calls
but she doesn't turn her head, if she hears him at all.

Ellen's room
is a sea, with a carpet of sand.
Dolphins leap, fish drift
and a mermaid sits on the coral chest,
combing her sea-green hair.

Ellen dives into the waves
as a wisp of spray
takes Jinnie away.

Jinnie Ghost! Jinnie Ghost!
Where do you go?

Owen dreams of bogeymen
as he curls up in bed with the sheet across his head.
"Will they get me tonight?"

Here come the bogeymen!
Yellow eyes stare
through the window,
in the mirror,
in the wardrobe,
on the pillow.
Shadows flicker everywhere.

"Where's the bogeyboy?"
they ask.

And while Owen boogies with the bogeyman
Jinnie melts away like wax.

Jinnie Ghost, Jinnie Ghost, the bogeymen call
but she doesn't turn her head, if she hears them at all.

Joe is dreaming giants.
His house shakes like paper.
Feet tramp
to the door
Tramp tramp
up the stairs
Tramp tramp
on the landing
Tramp tramp
in the bedroom.

Huge hands
lift him
high, high, high
and he rides the giant's shoulders
to his castle in the sky,
while far down below him
Jinnie Ghost slips by.

Jinnie Ghost! Jinnie Ghost! the giant roars
but she doesn't turn her head,
if she hears him at all.

She's a white owl flying
She's a deep river flowing
She's a thin wind sighing
casting dreams
through the night.

But the break of day takes her breath away
like sun on snow.

The children awake
brushing wonder from their eyes.

Jinnie Ghost, Jinnie Ghost,

Where do you go...?